"Do I Stink?"

A Littlest Coyote Story

NM Reed

&

McCarthy Preston

Illustrations- DaVinci ai sourced

www.TatteredUnicornPublishing.com

“Do I Stink?”

A Littlest Coyote Story

"Have a good day at school, Billy," said her mother.
"When you get home we have to talk about your puppy."

"What about my puppy!" said Billy. "Well," answered her mother, "for one thing you sister says he stinks and should stay outside."

Billy said to her sister, "You told mom that Coyote stinks?"
"Well, he does," replied her sister. "And soon, he'll have to live outside!"

While Billy was away at school that day, her sister told their mother, "I want him out of my room." And their mother replied, "And he needs to stay out of the kitchen, too,"

On her way home from school, Billy realized what her family had said about her puppy, the Littlest Coyote, and how it might hurt his feelings.

Billy was sad. She didn't want to tell Coyote what they had said about him.
She thought it might hurt his feelings.

"What's wrong Billy?" He could see that she was crying. "My mother and my sister said that you stink." "Oh, no! I stink!" he cried. "What's that mean?"

"But, Coyote, my mom and sister said the you stink.
Let's go out and ask all the animals, and see what they think!"

"Let's go ask the animals." So, Billy put some ranch clothes on, and she and the Littlest Coyote went out to the barn where all the ranch animals lived.

"Hi! I'm Ralph the ranch dog. I can show you around to all the animals. Wait! Let me get my hat!" said Ralph to Billy and Coyote.

When Ralph the ranch dog finally realized he already had his hat on his head, he said, "Well, let's go ask them critters and see if they think you stink."

The first farm animal they came to was old Mrs. Mother Cow and her calf.
"Hello, Mrs. Cow. Can you take a sniff and tell me, Do I stink?"

"No, Mr Dog. I don't think you stink. You smell just like a dog to me!"
said Mrs. Cow chewing her cud happily.

The mother cow was polite, saying he doesnt stink.
"I'll ask the baby cow , tell me, what do you think?"

"Would you please take a sniff?" he asked the baby calf. "Do I stink?"
The calf took a sniff. "You smell just like a puppy! That's what I think!"

He came to some chickens in the chicken yard. He told them to take
a sniff, and concentrate hard.

"Can you please take a sniff? It's not that hard,"
the Littlest Coyote asked the chickens in the chicken yard.

The chickens looked confused and looked away.
They didn't have time to talk to a dog all day.

He saw some chicks playing in the grass. "Do I stink? If I may ask." They pecked and they chirped and gave not a wink. And passed him by as he did not stink.

He wasn't too sure of those chickens he'd seen.
So, they walked some more till they came to a stream.

Some little ducklings then came past, with coyote sitting in the grass.
"So, if I asked you what you think, you'd walk right past if I did not stink?"

And then he had the best of luck. He came upon a little white duck. He said,
"Tell me little duck, can you tell me true? Tell me, do I stink, do I stink to you?"

"Well, little puppy, if you think you stink, why not come in and have a drink?"
And if you think you stink so bad, come on in and have a bath."

Then, two little goslings, they came by. They stopped to tell the Littlest Coyote "Hi!"
"Hey, little guys, tell me true. Do I stink to you?" The goslings said "Peep, peep."

There a little donkey sat so sweet. A thousand flowers at his feet. "Hey, little doggie, what a treat. I like for you my family to meet."

His wife and babe were there, too. Sniffing flowers, and Coyote, too.
"So, tell me, friends, what do you think? Do you think I really stink?"

"Could you give me a sniff, Mr. Flowers and see what you find."
Mr. Flowers bent down and sniffed his nose not behind.

"To lick my face, I didn't say. Just give it a sniff, see if I'm OK."
Donkey got close and gave it a wiff. A sniff and wiff in just one short jiff.

Then the donkey said, "Mr. Coyote, you don't stink to me."
And the Littlest Coyote smiled and thanked him, happy as can be.

"I'll tell if you stink you little dog. I rather think you look like a hog. But, as to whether I think you stink, compared to a hog, that's not what I think!"

He said to the goat,"You look like me! "Except for these great little horns you see."
Tell me, what do you think? Do you also not think I stink?"

"Now, don't you worry your cute little head, about what those silly kids said.
They are just silly kid boys. Run along now and play with your toys."

Along bounced a family of little bunnys.
They were cute, but to Coyote they just looked funny.

"Oh, Mr. Rabbit, I love your ears. Come over and sniff me, come over here."
"With these ears I can hear pretty good. But, I cant really sniff like a rabbit should."

Then, Mrs. Rabbit came hopping along.
"Come on, little babies, let's get home to the barn!"

"That doggie wants to know what we think. To see if his fur really does stink."
But, by now, they were tucked safe in their box, safe from the lion, tiger and fox.

"Let's go see the piglets and pigs!"
"We'll find them down in their muddy digs!"

The four little piglets came running up to the puppy sitting in the grass.
He told them, "There's something I would like to know, if I might ask?"

The smallest piglet came and sat by him there.
"My, aren't you fuzzy," he said. "You are covered with hair!"

"You're getting off subject," Coyote said with a whine.
"That's OK," said the piglet, "for I am only just swine."

The biggest little piglet came and sat by his side.
"You are cute and you do not stink and I think that is why."

He found the biggest pig in the wooden house for pigs.
It wasn't fancy, but for them, pretty nice digs.

"Hey, giant pig. You are so big and pink.
Do you think you could tell me, do you think I stink?"

"
Tell me, little dog. What do you think? Since I live in a barn
full of animals, could I tell if you stink?"

Then there was a momma sheep and her lamb. They said,
"hello, little doggie. Do you know what I am?"

"Yes, fuzzy one. You're a sheep. Come in close and sniff.
Do I stink?" "Oh, no you smell fine," said the sheep in a wink.

A big giant horse walked over and looked him in the eye.
"Say, giant horse, give me a sniff, can you give it a try?"

"Let's go find Billy and get out of the barn.
Out in the field where the sun is warm."

The big horse said to Billy, "I think he smells fine.
But, I'm g;lad that he's your dog because he's not mine."

Ranch Dog Ralph said, "I think that's a day! Maybe take a bath and hit the hay.
Let's tuck inside when the night gets chilly. So long for now, Coyote and Billy!"

The Littlest Coyote said with wet eyes, "I want to tell all of my friends, you've been so kind. For sniffing and answering, you are all friends of mine!"

"You're all such good friends, let's say our goodbyes.
Because, if I waits to long, I'm a gonna cries."

"I loves to howl, I'm the Littlest Coyote.
Let's say farewell, and Okie Dokie!"

As the Littlest Coyote and Billy were climbing into bed,
he asked her, "Billy, what would you have said?"

And Billy said softly as they were falling asleep,
"My little puppy, you smell like love to me."

And Billy and her puppy, the Littlest Coyote, drifted off to sleep,
to dream about their next adventure.

The Adventures of Elf and Troll: Two Kingdoms
by NM Reed with Whitney Lee Preston
Tattered Unicorn Publishing

book review by Joslyn Vann

"She took a bit of spark from her heart and held it out in front of her in the palm of her hand."

Although diminutive in size, Elf is a feisty wood elf and hunter who always outsmarts predators. On behalf of the Good Queen of the south, Valerie the Kind, Elf must journey to the Kingdom of Wisdom to deliver an important message to King Harold the Wise. Accompanying Elf is her protector—the often misunderstood Troll whose massive size, granite skin, extensive weaponry, and body armor make for an imposing figure. As the companions travel back and forth to establish communication between the two kingdoms, they endure many perils, encounter a diverse variety of creatures, and uncover a sinister plot with multiple sources of evil and villainy.

Married writing partners Reed and Preston collaborate to deliver this highly imaginative tale as the first installment in a series of eight fantasy adventures. The authors use a descriptive writing style and artistic imagery to draw readers into a world where the majesty of nature is on full display. One of the book's most powerful scenes is that of Elf using her love to make time stand still and then drawing a spark of magic from her own heart, creating a glowing display of sparkles glittering on the flakes of freshly fallen pure snow. The power of love and loyalty and the beauty of nature are recurrent themes throughout the book as Elf and Troll receive help and protection from nymphs, dryads, and mystical wolves. These elements of natural beauty and friendship provide a stark contrast to the dark forces of human jealousy and mythical creatures like worm walkers, spirit demons, dark forces enchanters, and evil fallen deities. In the end, Reed and Preston effectively set the stage for the next adventure of Elf and Troll.

Return to USR Home

N. M. Reed and McCarthy Preston are the dynamic authors
of dozens of titles. They live in Northern California on a ranch with lots of animals and books.

"Adventures of Elf and Troll" series 1-6
"The Adventures of Elf and Troll: The Tattered Unicorn" series 7-12
"The Oak Grove of Maeve"
"Worrisome War of the Whimsical Wizards" or "The Dueling Wizards of Simpletown"
"Worrisome War of the Whimsical Wizards2: Dungeon For Dollars"
Home is Where the Horse Is : A Safer Place a true story of fire survival
The Glass Planet science fiction series
"The Littlest Coyote" and its coloring book and 9 languages
The Littlest Coyote Christmas and its coloring book
The Littlest Coyote and the Spotted Unicorn and coloring book
The Littlest Coyote Gets Spring Fever
The Littlest Coyote and Flowers the Donkey
The Littlest Coyote and the Howling Halloween Pumpkin
The Littlest Coyote Falls in Love
The Tattered Unicorn now in 4 languages
Bartimon the Boy Wizard and the Golden Squirrel

Available on Amazon.com
Walmart.com
Walmart and BarnesandNoble.com
and NMReedBooks.com
TatteredUnicronPublishing.com